KU-391-030

£4.50

THIS BOOK
BELONGS TO

CONTENTS

THE END.

14

TOM & JeRRy GAME

You will need:
4 or 5 toilet roll tubes
A cardboard box
Some glue or sellotape
Some old newspaper

How you make your own game:
Tape or stick the toilet roll tubes onto the bottom of the upturned box. You can make each tube worth a different amount of points either by painting each tube a different colour or by writing its value on the side. Scrunch up the newspaper into little balls, and standing about 2 metres from the tubes, see if you are a better aim than Tom!

SPOT THE DIFFERENCE!
Can you spot the 10 differences between these two pictures?

16

TWO-FACED TOM

"Grr! Just lemme get my claws on you. . .!" scowled Tom, as he hurtled around the house in hot pursuit of Jerry.

"That'll be the day," chuckled the fleet-footed little mouse, leaping for the cuckoo clock. He squeezed inside and took cover.

"C'mon out, you rotten rodent!" called Tom, peering closely at the clock face. "Or are you scared I'll catch you?"

Even as Tom spoke, a small door opened in the front of the clock and the wooden cuckoo sprang out. Clinging to it, Jerry shot forward, too, right on to Tom's nose.

"Here I am and *bang* on time, Tom," laughed the mouse, "seeing as you're so keen to be *clocked*!"

As Tom staggered back, blinking hard, Jerry made no further attempt to flee. Instead, he stood on the arm of the sofa nearby, and wagged a finger at the flustered feline.

"Listen, Tom! What say I let you catch me all next week, if you behave like a perfect pal

of a puss and are real polite to my guest. He's due any time!"

"Guest?" muttered Tom, still rubbing his nose.

"Sure! My little nephew Tuffy," began Jerry. But a clattering at the front door interrupted him. "Ah! That must be him now!"

17

"Hi, Uncle Jerry!" called Tuffy, clambering through the low-slung letter-box, pulling a small case behind him. "It's real nice of you to let me come and stay!"

Before Jerry could answer, Tom leapt into action. But now he was not intent on a rodent-hunt. Instead, he raced for the vacuum cleaner and plugged it in.

"Why ever didn't you warn me, Jerry?" called Tom, with a broad smile. "A guest in our house, and we haven't even cleaned up properly. Leave this to me!"

"Reckon Tom's agreed to my deal," muttered Jerry in amazement.

"Wow! What a kind cat!" said Tuffy. "Isn't he good to help!"

VROOOP! There was a sudden sweep of the vacuum head, and the powerful suction pulled Tuffy into the cleaner's tubular body.

"Like you said, Tuffy!" chuckled Tom. "I'm helping myself. I'll clean up this place of mice, once and for all!"

"You treacherous Tom-cat!" protested Jerry. "You let poor little Tuffy out of there – and fast. Or else!"

"Whatever you say, rodent!" replied Tom, switching the vacuum cleaner to 'blow'. Next second, Tuffy flew out of the end amid dust, debris, and a high-powered blast. He landed on Jerry.

"You try catching your nephew, Jerry," laughed Tom. "Looks like I can catch out that pea-brained rodent any time I like! Ha-ha!"

"I'd sure like to teach that Tom a thing or two," said Tuffy, later, after he had recovered in the safety of Jerry's mousehole.

"I'll have to give you lessons in handling that treacherous Tom first, Tuffy!" replied Jerry.

"Yoo-hoo!" called Tom, in a sickly-sweet voice, as he crouched on the other side of the mousehole entrance. "I sure am sorry about my bad behaviour. What say we all make friends? Come out and play, Tuffy?"

Young Tuffy's face brightened. If there was one thing he liked, it was a good game. "I forgive you, Tom," he called. "I'm coming!"

"No, wait!" cried Jerry, jumping up to stop his unsuspecting nephew. But he was too late.

"Shall we play ball?" Tuffy turned hopefully to Tom, emerging into the living room.

"You said it, pal – baseball!" purred the cunning cat, as he brought a baseball bat crashing down, a whisker's width from Tuffy's tail.

"Yipes! Uncle Jerry! Heeelp!" yelled Tuffy, racing for cover. "That Tom tricked me!"

"It's time I showed him a trick or two," said Jerry, as he hurtled to the rescue. He saw Tom, on all fours, peering under an armchair where Tuffy was trapped. Unnoticed, Jerry fetched something from the hall cupboard and called to Tom from the doorway. "Like I was saying earlier, you furry freak, you couldn't

even catch a cold!"

"Is that so?" replied Tom, taking the bait. He spun round and ran, full-pelt, for Jerry, swinging the baseball bat as he went. "You'll be one minced mouse if you don't get your skates on! So step on it!"

But the rodent remained where he stood, leaning casually against the half-open door. It was only as the cat was a split-second away, that Jerry pushed something under Tom's raised foot. Instantly, Tom felt himself carried forward at a gathering pace.

"Waagh!" he yelled, hurtling into the hallway.

"Seems you've stepped on that skateboard!" chuckled Jerry. "I know you're having fun. But don't get too carried away!"

In fact, Tom was carried just as far as the front door. There was a loud thud and the sound of splintering

wood, as the cat connected with it. Then he slipped slowly down to floor level, a big bump appearing on the top of his head.

"I'm going to tell that bullying cat just what I think of him!" said Tuffy angrily, emerging from his hiding place. But, surprisingly, there was no need. No sooner had Tom opened his eyes, than he saw the rodent relatives and began to cry!

"Sob! Howl! You're just so cute! And so small! But don't you worry about a thing. I'm going to take care of you both!"

"You are?" repeated Jerry and Tuffy, puzzled.

"Starting right now!" smiled Tom, patting them both on the head. Jerry noticed Tom's eyes had a glazed,

faraway look. Then Tom hurried to the kitchen and returned with a plateful of cheese.

"Lunch is served. But why not watch the TV, too?" he suggested. "If you'll allow me to turn it on!"

"It must be that knock Tom took on his head," giggled Jerry, as he merrily munched on a morsel of cheese.

"Let's enjoy it," chuckled Tuffy. "He'll do anything we ask!"

Just to prove the point, Tuffy ordered Tom to tidy up the whole house, and the cat willingly set to work.

"Yep! We've really got him on the run!" added Jerry, watching Tom hurtling about, dusting, polishing, and wiping windows.

There was nothing Tom would not do for them. He fetched them cola and popcorn, and even ran all the way to the corner shop to rent a video for them to enjoy.

So it went on until neither Jerry or Tuffy could think of a single thing left for Tom to do. The two mice lay on the hearth-rug pondering the problem, while Tom hovered close-by, eager for orders.

"Perhaps I could cook you a nice cheese flan, or read you a story?" he began. "There must be something!"

"How about getting lost!" replied Jerry, finally losing patience. After all, too much of a good thing does wear rather thin.

Poor Tom was so shocked, his jaw fell open.

"Yeah! Do what you like," snapped Tuffy, "only just stop wet-nursing us. It's not natural!"

"Besides, it gets kind of boring!" agreed Jerry, who wished Tom was back to his troublesome self again.

"No, please, don't send me away!

I'll do anything. . . anything. . .!" pleaded the deranged cat, clasping his paws and stepping forward. Next moment, he tripped on the edge of the rug and went flying. He landed, with a resounding BONNNNG! against the grandfather clock. It swayed, but did not fall over. Tom copied its movements exactly. As his eyes rolled, another bump appeared beside the first on his head.

Jerry and Tuffy shook with laughter. "Now that's what I call entertainment. Tee-hee!" giggled one.

"You can . . . ha-ha! . . . do that again, if you like, Tom!" added the other.

But the smiles froze on their faces as the furious feline advanced, his arms full of fruit that he'd snatched up from a bowl. He began to hurl it all at the retreating mice.

"Grr! I can't remember a thing that's happened," said Tom. "But I sure know that chasing you rotten little rodents feels right!"

"I agree!" said Jerry. "Quick, Tuffy – head for home! That second bash on the head has turned Tom back to normal!"

"Mind if I go first?" puffed Tuffy, reaching the mousehole, a split-second before Jerry.

"Be my guest," said Jerry, diving in after him. "For the rest of your stay, it's safer if you just stay put!"

TOM'S TREASUR HUNT!

Help Tom recover the hidd treasure!

ow to play the game: You will
ed a dice and one counter per
ayer. The first player to throw a six
arts. If you land on a square with a fish
it, have another throw! But if you
nd on a square with one of the tips of
e octopus on it, then you have to go
ack to square **5** and start again!

WHAT SORT OF DRAGON DO YOU MEAN? WHAT DOES IT DO?

WELL, YOU CAN FLY IT!

GREAT! IT FLIES AWAY! AND THEN?

IT'S CRAZY! WHY BUILD A DRAGON THAT WILL JUST FLY AWAY!

YOU DON'T KNOW WHAT YOU'RE TALKING ABOUT! STUPID MICE!

I'LL SHOW YOU HOW YOU STOP IT FLYING AWAY!

ALWAYS GO AGAINST THE WIND! PULL A LITTLE ON THE STRING...UP IT GOES! HIGHER!

PROFILE »

TOM™

is always plotting and planning new ways to get the better of that little mouse, Jerry. His pranks have an amazing tendency to go wrong quite a lot of the time though...

JERRY™

is brilliant at baiting the hapless Tom and thwarting his best made plans. With his big ears and talent for moving fast, he always makes sure he's one step ahead of Tom...

WORDSEARCH

Jerry has managed to mix up all the names of Tom's favourite animals! Can you help him to find them all? They are hidden in the puzzle below, but beware! They can be spelt backwards, forwards, diagonally or anyway Jerry can think of to fool Tom!

H	A	T	E	E	H	C	A	M	I	M	G	G
I	L	A	B	L	N	A	H	K	A	I	N	O
P	V	O	K	E	C	M	J	O	R	E	C	R
P	Q	W	A	P	J	E	D	A	B	E	R	I
O	B	P	X	H	I	L	F	E	E	Z	O	L
P	F	G	R	A	H	F	P	K	Z	N	C	L
O	D	G	S	N	E	Y	A	E	L	A	O	A
T	T	Q	C	T	H	N	D	E	J	P	D	M
A	L	E	R	C	G	I	S	U	A	M	I	N
M	I	S	Z	A	V	R	J	B	G	I	L	R
O	O	K	R	F	O	W	L	Q	U	H	E	A
U	N	O	X	H	G	D	P	T	A	C	L	Z
S	O	R	E	C	O	N	I	H	R	Y	U	S

RHINOCEROS
ZEBRA ✓
LION ✓
CHEETAH
JAGUAR
KANGAROO
GIRAFFE

HIPPOPOTAMOUS ✓
ELEPHANT
CAMEL
CROCODILE
HORSE
GORILLA ✓
CHIMPANZEE

35

DOUBLE

Jerry is a wonderful instructor in the fine art of cat harassment, with Tuffy his talented pupil! Help Tom catch the mice and try to avoid their many tricks on the w

| 3 | 4 | 5 | IT GETS TOUGH LATER! 1 EXTRA THROW! | 6 | 7 |

2 AN EXTRA THROW!

START **1**

| 28 | 27 | GOOD SHOT, JERRY! MISS A GO, TOM! | 26 |

MISS A GO!

WELL DONE TOM! YOU'VE TAUGHT THE MICE A LESSON. EXTRA THROW.

31

| 35 | HA, HA! HOW ARE THEY GOING TO GET OUT OF THIS ONE? GO BACK 6! | 33 | "KICK ME" TRICK! MISS A GO! |

| 44 | GO BACK 5. | 46 |

43

"KICK ME" TRICK! MISS A GO!

36

JERRY + TUFFY RETURN THE MOUSE-TRAP. GO BACK 4!

| 37 | 38 | OH NO! NOT THE "KICK ME" TRICK. WELL, YOU'VE FALLEN FOR IT! GO BACK 6! | 40 | 41 |

TROUBLE!

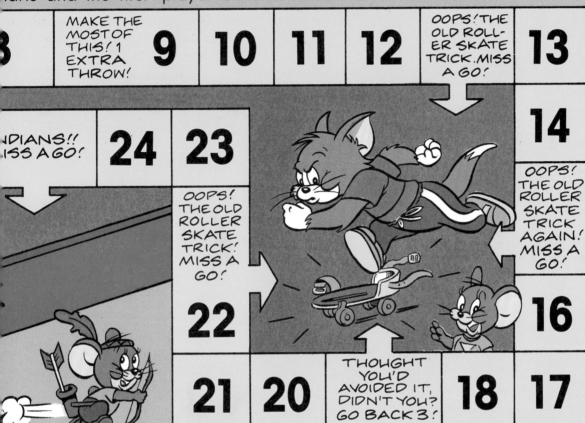

How to play the game: You will need a dice and ~~o~~ne counter per person. The first player to throw a six ~~s~~tarts and the first player to the finish catches the mice!

8	MAKE THE MOST OF THIS! 1 EXTRA THROW!	**9**	**10**	**11**	**12**	OOPS! THE OLD ROLLER SKATE TRICK. MISS A GO!

13

~~I~~NDIANS!! ~~M~~ISS A GO!

24 **23**

14

OOPS! THE OLD ROLLER SKATE TRICK! MISS A GO!

22

OOPS! THE OLD ROLLER SKATE TRICK AGAIN! MISS A GO!

16

21 **20**

THOUGHT YOU'D AVOIDED IT, DIDN'T YOU? GO BACK 3!

18 **17**

~~L~~OOK WHAT ~~T~~OM'S FOUND! ~~M~~ISS A GO!

48 **49**

50

OUCH! GO BACK 3!

51

52 **53** | FINISH

T O M'S CAT

"Jerry! J-E-R-R-Y!" yelled Tom, hurtling along the garden path. Jerry leapt out of the birdbath, where he had been enjoying a midday dip, and fled.

"Wait, I want to tell you something!" protested Tom. "Boy, have I got some news for you!"

"Let me guess!" replied Jerry, speeding across the lawn. "You told your feline friends you're gonna make mouse-meat of me!"

Jerry didn't wait for an answer, but headed at full-speed for the garden shed. He took a short-cut across the rose-bed. Being so small, he had no trouble avoiding the prickly stems. But would Tom, intent on the chase, follow him into the trap? The answer came in a series of anguished howls.

"A mouse-terly trick, eh, Tom?" laughed Jerry, diving through a large knot-hole in the shed door and taking cover beneath a flowerpot. As Jerry waited for Tom to come bursting in, he admitted to himself that there was nothing quite like the fun of a good old chase. Life would sure be dull if that tatty cat weren't around.

But, in fact, Tom was still not to be seen. Cautiously, Jerry emerged from his hiding place and peered out of the shed. He was just in time to see Tom heading into the house, pulling thorns from his fur.

"Suit yourself, Jerry!" Tom called. "But I'm through with our cat-and-mouse games. From now on, I'm a working cat!"

As if to prove the point, Tom packed an executive case then smartly slicked down his fur,

ASTROPHE!

before the hall mirror. Jerry could hardly believe his ears.

"Yep," continued Tom, opening the front door, "I've got me a really hot job in the high street! See you around, sometime!"

The mouse sighed sadly, as he sat on the gatepost and watched Tom stride purposefully down the road.

"I'm sure going to miss that cat," muttered Jerry, miserably. Then, suddenly, his face brightened. "But I won't, if I follow him into town. . ."

"Two mighty munch-burgers and double fries!" the burger bar manager called to Tom, who was dressed in a chef's hat and big, white apron. "And hurry it up. We're not even busy yet!"

Tom mopped his furry brow and tossed the burgers on to the hot-plate. He was beginning to have second thoughts about this being the best

job for a cat of his talents, despite being offered all the free fishburgers he could eat! A sudden torrent of orders from some newly-arrived customers confirmed Tom's doubts. Much as he'd never let on to Jerry, this was definitely no match for a mouse-hunt. Tom even found himself wondering just where Jerry was. . .

"Hi, Tom! What's cooking?" a familiar voice surprised him. Tom's eyes nearly shot from their sockets as he saw Jerry standing on the counter, right before him.

"GO AWAY!" hissed the cat. "Can't you see I'm working!" Jerry stared at Tom in amazement.

"Hey Tom! watch this!" Jerry stuck his tongue out at Tom and jumped up and down, trying desperately to goad the cat into chasing him.

"Excuse me, you pesky mouse!" shouted Tom, "but can't you see I'm working! I don't have time to chase any silly little rodents!"

"I don't believe it!" muttered Jerry, darting off to find some fun. "There must be some way to bring that dumb cat back to normal!"

"Shriek! A mouse!" screamed a woman in alarm. She leapt up, sending her strawberry milk-shake cascading over another customer. The cry was echoed and, in moments, there was a stampede to the door. The manager followed his customers into the street, trying to calm them.

Meanwhile, Tom advanced on Jerry, cornering him by a plate of chips. As the cat lunged, Jerry flipped the plate, so its greasy contents landed over Tom. "Looks like you've had your chips, tatty cat!" giggled Jerry, racing away again. But Tom was not to be put off. Both cat and mouse skidded this way and that, round and round the kitchen, until Tom finally pulled off his chef's hat and brought it down over Jerry.

With a triumphant leer, Tom hooked Jerry out by his tail and headed for the hot-plate.

"I . . . er . . . take my hat off to you, Tom. That sure was a smart move," said Jerry, uneasily. "Guess the heat's really on me now, eh?"

"It will be, pal – any time at all," replied Tom, reaching for a plastic sauce bottle, with his free paw. "I'll just add a little seasoning, then it's one mighty mouse-burger coming up. Heh-heh!"

"Hold it, Tom!" called Jerry, still dangling in mid-air from his tail. He pointed to the sauce bottle and frowned. "Don't use that bottle. It's blocked!"

"It is?" said Tom, holding one end of it up to his eye to get a closer look.

"Just fooling!" giggled Jerry, as he swung towards the bottle, then squeezed it hard as he could. SPLOOP! A jet of bright-red sauce hit Tom full in the face. Shocked, he staggered back, releasing the mouse – and momentarily rested on the hot-plate. SSSSVVVZZ! The sound of singeing fur was followed by an ear-piercing howl.

"Reckon that cat's not so cool now!" laughed Jerry, enjoying this burger bar chase more than any they'd had at home. Tom, though, was intent upon revenge. Snatching up a pile of burger buns, he hurled them after the amused mouse.

"Looks like Tom's really turning this into a bun-fight!" said Jerry, twisting and weaving to avoid the missiles. Next, followed a barrage of doughnut-rings.

"Grr! I'll run rings round you, rodent!" roared Tom.

Jerry returned fire with a salvo of pickled onions, plucked from a big jar nearby. Even as Tom released the last of the doughnut-rings, he gave a full-blooded cat-cry: "Charrrrrge!"

But an airborne onion found its target. Tom's mouth slammed shut as the onion hit the back of his throat. His eyes rolled and he gulped.

"I'm still waiting, Tom!" called Jerry, leaning confidently against a cola bottle. "Or have I made you swallow your words?"

But while Jerry spoke, a flying doughnut-ring landed clean over both rodent and bottle. Jerry was

trapped against it as surely as if he'd been tied. All he could do was hop helplessly, shaking the bouncing bottle as he went.

Tom's throat felt almost as scorched as his tail-end. He speedily snatched up Jerry and the cola bottle. Without waiting to free the mouse, Tom began to unscrew the top.

"Thirsty work, catching me, eh, Tom?" teased Jerry.

Tom's throat was burning too much to speak. The bottle-top was almost free . . .

struck Spike. He was soaked!

All Tom could manage was a sickly grin. But, at the sound of Spike's threatening, throaty growl, the cowardly cat suddenly took fright!

"You're fired!" howled the burger bar manager, by the door.

"I quit!" screeched Tom, speeding past.

Spike looked as if he'd been fired, too – from a gun! He hurtled after Tom, leaving a bemused Tyke and

At that same moment, Spike 'n' Tyke entered the burger bar.
"What say we have a burger before the ball-game, son!" Spike told Tyke. "And maybe a nice, cook drink, too?"

Simultaneously, Tom looked round in horror as the bottle-top came off in his paw. VROOOOSH! Like a high-powered hose, the fizzy cola – so recently shaken up by Jerry – gushed across the burger bar and

Jerry watching.

"Guess we may as well enjoy these burgers, Tyke," said Jerry, noticing two still sizzling on the hot-plate. "I don't think Tom'll want them now."

As they both left the burger bar, munching merrily, they could just make out the distant figures of Tom and Spike. Jerry giggled. "Reckon Tom's doing his best to steer clear of that hot-dog, too! Tee-hee!"

PICNIC POACHERS!

Help Tom to find his picnic before Jerry and Tuffy eat the lot!

PARK

43

How to play the game: You will need a dice and four of each of these coloured counters — red, yellow, green and blue. You must throw a six to take one of your counters out of base. You must work your way round the board with each counter until your reach the **HOME** stretch

LUDO GAME!

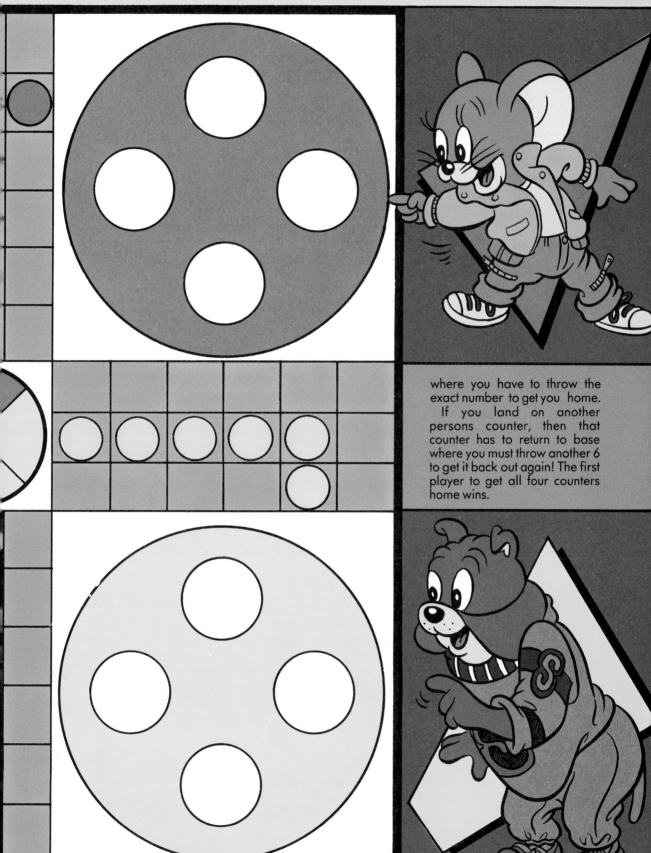

where you have to throw the exact number to get you home. If you land on another persons counter, then that counter has to return to base where you must throw another 6 to get it back out again! The first player to get all four counters home wins.

Gamble.

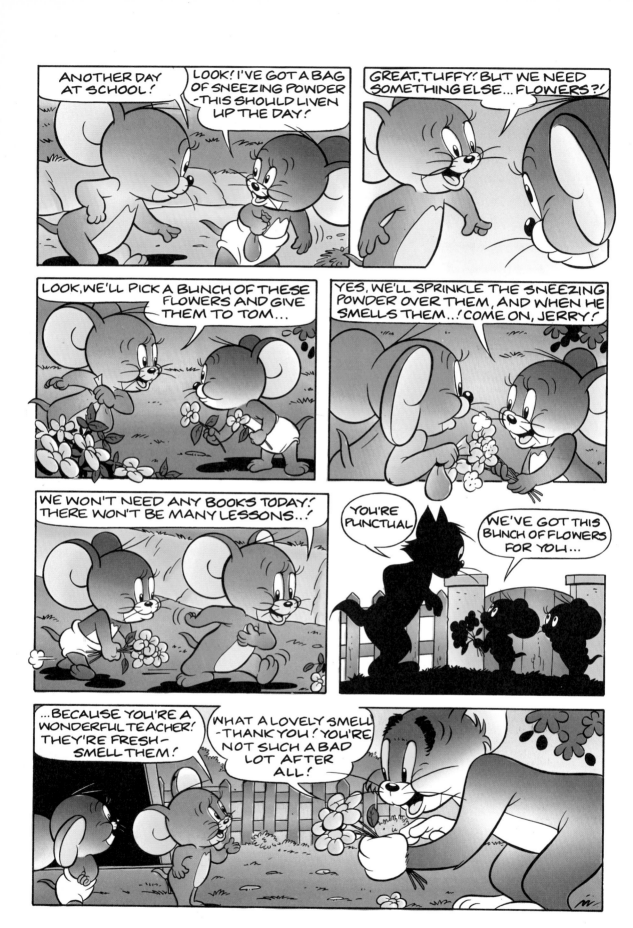

54

star struck!

"Gah! C'mere! You're gonna be one minced mouse!" yelled Tom, as he chased Jerry across the kitchen. Thud! Thump! THUNK! A split-second after Jerry darted away, Tom brought the rolling-pin crashing down behind him.

"You're mousetaken, Tom! You'll never pin me down! Chuckle!"

Jerry dived for cover in a cupboard, where he spotted a feather duster. It gave him an idea. As Tom crouched low and suddenly pulled open the cupboard door, Jerry appeared.

"You win this game of cat-and-mouse, Tom!" he said. "Go ahead – do your worst!"

"Huh?" gasped Tom, delighted. "You said it, pal!" Leaning forward, Tom raised the rolling-pin ready to strike. The next moment, Jerry snatched up the feather duster and tickled Tom under his arm.

"Ha-ha-hee-hee!" roared Tom, helplessly, so he was unable to stop himself swinging downwards and striking his own foot with the rolling-pin. But as Jerry continued to tickle him, Tom could only laugh and laugh, above his pain.

"I'm tickled pink this plan worked so well!" grinned Jerry. "It'd sure be no laughing matter if it hadn't!"

Knock! Knock! Above Tom's humorous howling, Jerry heard this new sound, as if Tom were tapping with the rolling-pin. But that lay on the floor now where he had dropped it.

Only then, did Jerry realise someone was at the front door. As he went to answer it, he left Tom recovering from his unwanted fit of the giggles.

"Er, you must be Jerry – the famous mouse!" said a man, bending down to shake his hand.

"And that must be Tom, the cat! Boy, this is a real pleasure! Am I glad I caught you both in!"

"You are?" asked Jerry, puzzled.

"Sure!" nodded the man. "And so will you be! I'm Ivor Scream, the TV producer! How would you two guys like your own show?"

"Y'mean us, appear on television – together?" gasped Jerry.

At last, Tom had stopped laughing and now stared in disbelief.

"Sure! Why not! You'll be a great hit! I mean, I heard all the laughter. You fellas must be great buddies!"

"Oh, er, purrrrrrfect pals!" agreed Tom, with a sickly smile, as

he patted Jerry on the head. "We're the best of friends, I mean, I never want to let Jerry out of my sight!"

"Sure!" added Jerry. "That cat is like a big bully . . . I mean, brother to me!"

"Then it's agreed!" said Ivor Scream, spinning on his heels. "You guys could end up with your own TV series. See you both at the studios tomorrow for your 'live' interview!"

"If Jerry lives that long!" muttered Tom under his whiskers, as the producer disappeared down the path. Tom had snatched up the rolling-pin again and was ready to strike.

"N. . . not so fast, cat-brain!" cried Jerry. "This is our big break! Remember? Our own coast-to-coast show! We'll be wealthy beyond our wildest dreams!"

"Yeah! You're right, Jerry!" said Tom, with a leer. "I'll have me fresh fish for every meal and be waited on paw and foot!"

"And I'll munch through a mountain of cheese each day!" added Jerry, dreamily. "Think of it, Tom! We'll be rich, RICH!"

"Then it's a truce, li'l' pal!" said Tom, sticking out a paw.

"Shake on it!" nodded Jerry. "From now on we need each other!"

Next day, a stretch-limo arrived to collect the two pet pals and drive them to the studio. As they arrived, press cameras flashed and Tom and Jerry soon found themselves signing paw-tographs for fans who flocked to see them.

As Tom suddenly flashed a sharp claw, Jerry felt uneasy. But Tom just dipped it into a bottle of ink to write his name for yet another admirer.

Ivor Scream rushed to greet them, yelling, "Make up!"

"But we haven't fallen out!" said Jerry.

"Nope!" nodded Tom. "Like we said, we're best buddies. Er, do we still get our own show?"

"I meant, it's time for your make-up!" laughed Ivor, ushering Tom and Jerry into the studio complex. "All stars must be made up to go on TV!"

And from make-up they were both whisked off to the wardrobe department, before finally being settled in chairs, beside each other, on the studio set, under the dazzling glare of the spotlights.

"Ready, take one – action!" called Ivor – and the cameras began to roll. As they did, Tom pulled his chair closer to them.

"Hi, there – you folks at home! I'm sure you wanna get a real close-up view of me, being such a famous feline!"

"Hey, don't forget li'l' me!" said Jerry, jumping down from his chair and pushing it closer, so it accidentally ran over Tom's tail.

Tom's grin turned to a grimace and he snatched up Jerry in his paw.

"Psst!" whispered Jerry. "Remember we're on air, Tom!"

For a moment, Tom struggled to ignore an imaginary picture of a juicy Jerry-filled sandwich. "Yes, folks," he continued into the cameras, "as I was saying. . .!"

This time, Tom popped Jerry into his jacket pocket.

"Steal the limelight, would you, you furry freak!" fumed Jerry, clambering out. "Well, it's time to really show who's boss between us!"

Jerry sprinted up on to Tom's shoulder and from there leapt for an overhanging microphone.

"Hi, folks! I may be small but I sure like to make myself heard!" As

Jerry yelled into the microphone, it made Tom's fur stand on end, especially when the mike slipped and struck him neatly on his nose.

"That does it!" shrieked Tom. "Jerry, you're history!"

In a moment, everything in the studio was flying – including Tom and Jerry – as Tom gave chase and they both hurled anything within reach at each other.

"Cut! CUT!" yelled Ivor while the show's presenter mumbled apologies to the viewers. "The show – it's ruined!"

So was most of the studio's equipment by the time Tom and Jerry paused, puffing and panting, for a brief rest.

"Listen, Jerry . . . what say we bury the hatchet again?" said Tom. "I guess I did kind of over-react!"

"Right, Tom!" nodded Jerry. "Let's you and me face the cameras together! We sure don't want to upset the viewers!"

It was only as they saw the fuming face of a seething Ivor Scream who advanced towards them, that they realised they had more than upset him, too!

"S. . . sorry, Ivor. We d. . .didn't mean t. . .to!" began Jerry, back-stepping until he bumped into Tom.

"S. . .sure, Mister Scream," added Tom, uneasily. "Just a little misunderstanding. It's all f. . . forgotten. Right, Jerry?"

"Wrong, Tom!" yelled Jerry, as Ivor snatched up a microphone stand and furiously rushed towards them. "Looks like he's pulled the plug on our TV show! Let's get outta here – fast!"

Hurtling home, the cat and mouse were back to business as usual – with Tom hot on Jerry's tail around the house.

"It's all your fault, you rotten little rodent!" screamed the cat. "We could've been superstars!"

The next moment Tom was seeing stars as Jerry pushed a plant pot down from a shelf on to his head.

"You were the cat-astrophe!" accused Jerry, racing on into the living room. "If you hadn't been so keen to take centre-stage!"

While Tom painfully picked pieces of plant, shattered pot and earth from his fur, it gave Jerry just the time he needed. When Tom followed him into the room, bent on revenge, Jerry was leaning casually against one of the legs of the television stand.

Tom advancing menacingly then, suddenly, he lunged. But Jerry just neatly side-stepped – and the leg of the television stand gave way, thanks to the screws the mouse had mischievously removed.

KER-ASSSH! The full weight of the television landed on Tom, who remained dazed and burbling beneath it. Jerry giggled, heading off for his mousehole home.

"Maybe you didn't get to be on TV, Tom," chuckled Jerry, happily. "But now the TV's on you! Tee-hee-hee!"